Henry E. Manning

Towards Evening

extracts from the writings of cardinal manning. Second Edition

Henry E. Manning

Towards Evening
extracts from the writings of cardinal manning. Second Edition

ISBN/EAN: 9783337264529

Printed in Europe, USA, Canada, Australia, Japan

Cover: Foto ©Andreas Hilbeck / pixelio.de

More available books at **www.hansebooks.com**

TOWARDS EVENING

A

SECOND EDITION

TOWARDS EVENING

EXTRACTS FROM THE WRITINGS

OF

CARDINAL MANNING

LONDON
KEGAN PAUL, TRENCH & CO.
1, PATERNOSTER SQUARE
1889

THIS LITTLE BOOK OF MAXIMS

IS DEDICATED

IN ALL HUMILITY

TO

THE ARCHCONFRATERNITY

OF THE

SERVANTS OF THE HOLY GHOST OF
S. MARY OF THE ANGELS,

BAYSWATER,

BY THE COMPILER.

A. M. W.

THE speedy sale of the First Edition has induced the Compiler to complete a series of Extracts for every day of the year.

TOWARDS EVENING.

January 1.

NAMES are realities; what they express is no mere sound, but a living truth. The Father is no mere sound, but a living Truth. The Father is the Father, not because He is called so, but He is called so because He is the Father. The Son is the Son, not because He is called the Son, but He is called so because He is the Son. Names stand by persons, and persons are living and real.

January 2.

LIFE is very short, and the world to come already dawns upon us. Choose boldly a life devoted to Christ. Be His above all; be His only. Hear the Church saying, "My Beloved is mine, and I am His."

January 3.

BE sure that in God alone can the deep cravings of our immortal being find enough. He has so made man's heart for Himself that it is ever restless until it finds rest in Him.

————

January 4.

WHAT we are is a revelation of God's Will towards us. Our lot is a reality. The works of our calling, so long as they are done as a service of obedience, are real. Within these bounds there is nothing which does not bear upon eternity.

January 5.

WE make our little cares, our common duties, our trade, or our profession a plea for shortening our devotions, or leaving our conscience unexamined, or postponing our confession. S. Charles worked always, and he prayed always; for his prayer and his work were one.

———

January 6.

O BLESSED Vision, to see God in Himself, to see Him in us, and ourselves in Him; with blissful joy, and joyful bliss, to sit at that feast ineffable, "where Thou, with Thy Son and the Holy Ghost, art unto Thy Saints true light, perfect fulness, everlasting joy"!

January 7.

EVERY day we might attain we know not what ; every day, it may be, loses or wins something of the brightness of the Resurrection.   All we do or leave undone has its counterpart in the unseen world ; and what then is life, and what is the world, to that day, when the Son of man shall sit on the throne of His glory? Forsake all, rather than forfeit your reward, rather than be set far off from Him when He cometh in to order the guests that are bidden to the marriage supper of the Lamb.

———

January 8.

HABITS form the character, and the character forms the countenance. God made the features, but each man makes his countenance.

January 9.

THE Catholic Church has, from the beginning, cherished and preserved the Holy Scriptures with the most vigilant and jealous care. The Saints of God have manifested their love for it with every token of veneration. S. Charles never read it except with his head bare, and upon his knees. S. Edmund of Canterbury kissed the page whensoever he opened the book, and kissed it again when he closed it. In this way the Saints of the Church have revered the Holy Scriptures.

January 10.

REMEMBER that you are immortal; realize your own immortality. Remember it all day long, in all places; live as men whose every act is ineffaceably recorded, whose every change may be recorded for ever.

January 11.

WE know that friends who love one another become like to each other; they catch the very tones of each other's voices; they exchange the very look of each other's countenances; features the most dissimilar acquire a strange likeness in expression. So it is with our souls, if we live in the habit of prayer; that is, of conversing and of speaking with our Divine Friend. They who live a life of prayer are being ever changed into the likeness of their Divine Lord. There is a gentleness, a sweetness, a kindness, a lowliness, an attraction about their life which makes everybody at peace with them.

January 12.

THERE are two things of which the world would fain rid itself: of the Day of Judgment, and the Sacrament of Penance. Of the former, because it is searching and inevitable ; of the latter, because it is the anticipation and the witness of the judgment to come.

––––––

January 13.

IN all that befalls us, we are not our own, but His; all that we call ours is His ; and when He takes it from us—first one loved treasure, then another, till He makes us poor and naked and solitary—let us not sorrow that we are stripped of all we love, but rather rejoice that God accepts us ; let us not think that we are left here, as it were, unseasonably alone, but remember that, by our bereavements, we are in' part translated to the world unseen. He is calling us away, and sending on our treasures.

January 14.

POVERTY is full of potent virtues. It is a sort of discipline, the ascetic rule of God's providence. They that are poor are already and unconsciously under a discipline of humility and self-denial.

————

January 15.

As the hammer welds the iron into a closer mass, so the indissoluble unity of the Catholic Church is, by persecution, tested, confirmed, and revealed. For eighteen centuries the mystical vine has stood, a living tree, rising in its stature, spreading in its reach, unfolding its leaves, multiplying its fruits, showing its imperishable vitality in every branch and in every spray.

January 16.

BEAR your witness for the sanctity of God in the world which is around you. Fear nothing but to be found on the world's side when He who redeemed us from it shall appear.

January 17.

ONWARDS and upwards! Onwards against the resistance, both within and without, which hinders our advance in the life of God; onwards without fear, or doubt, or wavering. And upwards, aiming as high as we can; for we have to ascend the mountains of the Lord's House, which are very high.

January 18.

PEACE in God is also a union with God —a consciousness that only God is enough for our happiness, and that God alone is enough without any other; and in this consciousness of attainment there is great rest. "In this peace I will sleep and take my rest."

January 19.

EVERY trial is sent to teach us something, and all together they have a lesson which is beyond the power of any to teach alone. But if they came together, we should break down, and learn nothing.

January 20.

WEALTH ill gotten soon perishes; goods heaped up by unrighteousness waste away; storehouses filled in forgetfulness of God are soon emptied; riches not sanctified by alms eat themselves through; worldly carefulness is a spendthrift, after all.

January 21.

WE are not what we seem to others, nor what we think ourselves, but what we are before God; and neither more nor less.

January 22.

THE habit of mind, which I will call the Catholic spirit, has five signs or rules, which will be found in a true Catholic student. They are—loving submission to the Church; devotion to the Saints; deference to theologians; fear and suspicion of novelty; mistrust of self.

January 23.

THE world's kisses are death to the hidden life.

January 24.

LET us learn how precious are solitary places, and hours when others are sleeping or away in the night season; or a great while before day, when the earth and heaven are still, and the busy world has not yet come abroad to trouble the creation of God.

January 25.

S. PETER, after he had wept bitterly for his three denials, entered upon a life of reparation to his Divine Master, which had its proportionate end and crown in his inverted cross. Such was the spirit of reparation among the disciples of Jesus —free, spontaneous, unsparing, even unto death.

January 26.

I KNOW there is no one that I know as I know myself, and no man knows me as I know myself, and though I may see other men commit many sins, yet I never see any man commit so many as I can number in myself.

January 27.

LET us learn not to go out of our lot and character in life, but to live above it. What and where we are is God's appointment. It is He Who makes us to joy or weep, to have or to lose. We have a work to do for Him, and it is just that work which lies before us in our daily life.

January 28.

THE busiest life may be a life of prayer ; perpetual toil need bring no hindrance to the union of the will with God.

January 29.

LESSER sins against greater light are more formally sinful than greater sins against lesser light.

January 30.

WHENSOEVER you have to choose between the maxims of the world and the counsel of your conscience, which comes to you from the Spirit of God, and from the holy faith, and in every doubt dictates to you what to do, choose the safe way of the Cross.

———

January 31.

LET us beware how we give much care or thought to anything but to the perfecting of our hidden life. What else is worth living for? What else shall endure at Christ's coming? Let us live ever waiting for that hour.

February 1.

FOR what else were we born, and for what end came we into the world, but to behold the Face of God ?   This is the end for which we were created.   To love God and to die—this is the end of man ; or read it in the light of heaven, to love God and to dwell in God for ever—this is our being and our bliss.

———

February 2.

HE who has not love and veneration for the Blessed Mother of Jesus is unlike our Divine Saviour in that particular perfection of His character, which comes next after His filial piety towards God.   As soon as a man receives into his heart the full light of the Incarnation, two self-evident truths arise upon his reason—the one, the Presence of Jesus in the Blessed Sacrament ; the other, the love and veneration of His Blessed Mother.

February 3.

WE never have more than we can bear. The present hour we are always able to endure. As our day, so is our strength. God sends first one trial, then another; then removes both, and lays on a third, heavier, perhaps, than either; but all is so wisely measured to our strength, that the bruised reed is never broken.

February 4.

A WILL elevated and inflamed with the love of God is so conformed to the will of God, that, as the shadow follows the substance, so it follows every motion of God's will in all the manifold wisdom of His ways.

February 5.

NEVER do we so put off the paint and masquerade of life as when we are alone under the Eye which seeth in secret.

February 6.

THE Church sits calmly in the see of truth, with a luminous universality and unity of faith confounding the multitudinous contradictions of error. It is a witness visible to the eye, audible to the ear, authoritative to the intelligence, and, as the Vatican Council says, "the irrefragable proof of its own Divine legation."

February 7.

EVIL men, evil lives, evil examples, spread a moral pestilence openly and powerfully; but nothing spreads falsehood and evil more surely and deeply than a bad book. A bad book is falsehood and sin in a permanent and impersonal form; all the more dangerous because disguised, and tenacious in its action upon the soul.

February 8.

THE love of God does not destroy, but elevates and perfects all other love to kindred and to friends. But it subordinates every affection to Him. It makes us not indifferent, but independent.

February 9.

OUR life is too continually outward and visible, and pent up in the throng of men. We are not enough at large and alone with God.

———

February 10.

IT is confusion to say that in all religions there is truth. Religion is one, not many; and the one only religion imperishably pervades the darkest aberrations of the human intellect; it has been, and is universal at all times, and amongst all the races of mankind.

———

February 11.

IF crosses, or contradictions, or troubles come, do not murmur or chafe against them; take them calmly, and accept them thankfully.

February 12.

In the measure in which we love God, in that measure we shall have more heart-felt love to all that are about us. A father will be a better father, and a mother a better mother; son and daughter will be better children; they will love each other more, and friends will love one another more, in the measure in which they love God more.

February 13.

The longest life, how short! The fairest earthly bliss, how poor! A few short years, and all will be over. Then there shall be no more sin and jar, no more infirmity and imperfection; then we shall have the power to taste of bliss, and to endure the taste.

February 14.

No man yet came to beggary by giving alms ; no man was ever yet made poor by a holy prodigality ; for, by the act in which he impoverished himself, he laid God under the pledge, sealed seven times, to restore to him in abundance that which He gave according to His promise.

February 15.

If we were Saints, if we loved God with all our soul and with all our strength, the most blessed day in life would be the last.   To go and be with Him Whom our soul loveth, to be for ever with Him, gazing upon His Face of love, ourselves sinless, and living by love alone,—this is heaven.

February 16.

S. GERTRUDE once heard these words in vision, "My child, there are many more saved than thou thinkest for ; I condemn no one who does not wilfully resist My grace."

February 17.

IT is only in Christ that we can find rest. It is only by learning of Him, yielding ourselves up to Him and living for Him, that we can find release from the causes of our disquiets, or rest for the deep cravings of an immortal being.

February 18.

WE see only a part of each other, but God sees all. Our partial view is, if not mingled with untruth, yet misleading, because imperfect ; we know only half the riddle, and we are led astray in guessing at the rest. " But all things are naked and opened unto the eyes of Him with Whom we have to do."

———

February 19.

THE sinfulness of sin consists not only in the specific evil of each particular act, but in the whole of our case before God ; in our relation to Him, His holiness, compassion, and long-suffering ; in His dealings with us, and our ingratitude, coldness, insensibility, in return.

February 20.

OUR share in the Beatific Vision will be according to our merit, and our merit will be according to our charity.

February 21.

How often have we asked for things which afterwards we see, if they had been given us, would have been our destruction ! Happily for us, there is interposed a wise and loving will between our prayers and their fulfilment.

February 22.

THE holiness of children is the very type of saintliness; and the most perfect conversion is but a hard and distant return to the holiness of a child.

February 23.

PERSONAL service is the best and most pleasing gift we can offer to our Lord in His poor. It is better than gold and silver. To give time, care, and sympathy in the miserable homes of the poor, is the best oblation we can make to Him, Who gave Himself for us.

———

February 24.

THEY are oftentimes the little ministries of love that show most devotion, and most intimate resolution of heart. Peter's worldly all was a boat and a net; and the alabaster box of ointment had a great testimony of acceptance, because "she had done what she could."

February 25.

A JOY in crosses may be of three kinds. First, those that are deserved for our faults, for our imperfections, and for our past sins. Secondly, those we have not deserved—as false accusations, contempt, and hatred without a cause. Thirdly, those that are voluntary ; that is, incurred by any acts or restriction of our liberty, which may offend those who indulge their liberty too much.

February 26.

TRY everything, measure everything, check everything, by the governing law of Christ's example. Seek first what is His ; and He will take care for what is your own.

February 27.

You are guilty in the measure in which you have greater light : in that measure in which you have a fuller illumination, in that measure your guilt before God is greater.

February 28.

There is only one person in the world to whom we may be severe. There is one who deserves it ; and we may vent all our severity on that person—and that person is our own self.

February 29.

No ignorance of truth is a personal sin before God, except that ignorance which springs from personal sin.

March 1.

ALL works of charity are good, but the surest and best of all are two : the education of children and of priests. Our Blessed Lord formed twelve men, and they created the Christian world, in all its fertility and multiplication of supernatural fruits. He has bequeathed to us all the continuance of this work.

——

March 2.

A LAX life has many sorrows, but a strict life has many joys.

March 3.

A LOVE of self is, in truth, the very soul of sin. All sins are but as circles issuing out from this one productive centre, expanding some more and some less widely, enclosing a narrower or a larger field of our spiritual life.

––––––

March 4.

The flattery, the adulation, the sycophancy with which people will wait upon the world to catch its favour, to be admitted into society, to sit at the tables of rich men, to be known as the acquaintance of those who bear titled names,—where this reigns in a man's heart, he is not the disciple of Jesus Christ.

March 5.

EVERY visitation is a state of advance in your walk of faith. Every chastisement is sent to open a new page in the great Book of Life—to show you things within you which you knew not, and things which hereafter shall be your portion. Welcome sorrow, trial, fear, if only our sin be blotted out, and our lot secure in the lowest room, in the light of His Face, before the throne of His beauty, in our home and in our rest for ever.

March 6.

THERE are three things to avoid in Confession. (1) Multiplicity of subjects. Keep rather to one sin. Confess it well with circumstances. (2) Avoid all irrelevance, everything that does not belong to the Confessional. (3) Keep from all human thought.

————

March 7.

Go through the world unnoticed if you can. Secret privations, secret sacrifices of your own will, which will never be known until all things are revealed, are surer instruments of perfection than chains and shirts of hair. The Holy Ghost in this way creates His Saints.

March 8.

ANTICIPATE the Day of Judgment. Be beforehand with it. That day is coming, inevitably coming, as the rising of to-morrow's sun. The day is not far off when the Great White Throne will be set up, and we shall stand before God, and the eyes that are as a flame of fire will search us through and through; and not His eyes alone, but the eyes of all men will be upon us, and the ears of men will hear that which the accuser will say against us in that day. There will be no secrecy then; no hiding of our sins; nothing con- cealed from God, or from that multitude which is around the Great White Throne.

March 9.

TAKE up your cross boldly; follow Jesus Christ. Have no compromises, no reserves, and He will do the rest for you.

_____

March 10.

S. PAUL of the Cross used to say to those about him, " Stay at home and keep three lamps always burning before the altar—faith, hope, and charity—before the presence of God in your heart."

_____

March 11.

CHRISTIAN matrimony is a Sacrament, and creates an indissoluble bond, which death alone can loose. The indissoluble bond of marriage is the fountain of the domestic life of Christendom.

March 12.

HUNT down and slay your little faults. " He that is faithful in that which is the least, is faithful also in that which is greater ;" and they who will hunt down, and slay, and exterminate their little faults, be sure of it, will never willingly commit greater sins.

———

March 13.

FASTINGS, disciplines, watchings, and the like, are nothing before God unless there be a true inward denial of self—a mortification of the intellect and heart and will. You remember the vision of S. Antony. The tempter came to him and said, " Antony, you fast a great deal, but I never eat ; you watch, but I never sleep ; you mortify the body, but I have no body to mortify ; but you do one thing I cannot —I cannot obey."

March 14.

EVERY single act of resisting temptation obtains merit and reward in the sight of God ; and they who are the most tempted obtain the most merit, if they faithfully resist ; so that the life that is harassed and buffeted with temptations without ceasing, if we persevere, is laying up perpetually more and more of merit before God, and more and more of reward in eternal life.

————

March 15.

WE have to learn not only our sins, but our personal sinfulness, our unworthiness, our unprofitableness, our littleness, and our weakness.

March 16.

IF you are suffering pains of body, unite them with the sufferings of Jesus Christ upon His Cross. If you have mental pains, sorrows of mind, trials of your family, ingratitude of friends, disobedience of children, the loss of those dear to you, whatsoever it be, unite them with the mental sorrows of Jesus dying upon the Cross.

————

March 17.

THERE is many a sorrow fearfully hidden from the world's hard gaze, many an overlooked affliction, many a piercing of heart by the sharpness of our common griefs, which not the less, when borne in silence, make the mourning spirit to partake of our Lord's mysterious Cross.

March 18.

EVERY theatre is the centre of a neigh-
bourhood abounding in all manner of evil,
which lives and thrives upon the theatrical
world. There are upon the stage many
good men, and many good women ; but
also of both, many bad. The spirit and
surroundings and tide of the stage are
dangerous, and downward. The classes
and trades that thrive by it are too well
known to need words from me. Why
should any one aid, abet, comfort, or share
in such a traffic, even by the price of a
box, or of a single ticket? I had rather
have no liability, however limited, in such
a trade. The money liability can be
limited, the moral cannot. If all things
are lawful, all are not expedient or edifying. Use your liberty for our Lord, as
He used His liberty for you.

March 19.

THERE are no illusions in the sight of
the Cross; all the colours and shadows,
the false play and changeful hues, the
gloss and the glitter which we put upon
ourselves in the sight of the world, and
even in the light of our own conscience,
are there overwhelmed by the direct and
all-revealing splendour of His presence.

———

March 20.

THE Cross becomes sweet when it is
chosen, and light when it is lifted on the
shoulder.

March 21.

TAKE the crucifix in your hand, and ask yourselves whether this is the religion of the soft, easy, worldly, luxurious days in which we live; whether the crucifix does not teach you a lesson of mortification, of self-denial, of crucifixion of the flesh.

———

March 22.

CAST up how much you spend in needless things, on things not wisely chosen, on things that perish in the using, on things that are not edifying to others, and not expedient for yourselves. How much is wasted, and worse than wasted, in these soft days of self-indulgence, in baubles, excitement, and ostentation !

March 23.

THERE is one sign of a true penitent : a willingness to be humbled, to bear shame before men as well as before God ; to go alone into the presence of men and angels, with no excuses or diminutions, no inculpations of others, or mitigating pleas.

———

March 24.

WHAT is a little while ? A little more sickness, sorrow, mourning, and solitude ; a little more of striving and persevering. A little while is soon over ; and then we shall be changed into a changeless joy. Then "we shall see Him as He is." What, then, is "a little while," if in a little while we may see Him for ever ?

March 25.

THE Blessed Virgin was exempted from original sin, and prepared to be the sanctuary of God in the Incarnation ; and surely the least grace proportionate to the Divine maternity is that she should be without sin.

———

March 26.

IN the heart there are so many windings and doubles, so many masks and disguises, so many false lights, so much paint upon the face, and so many artificial expressions of countenances, that it is certain we deceive ourselves as well as others. We must, therefore, be always pressing onwards in the knowledge of self, with much self-mistrust, and with a sincere desire to know the worst of ourselves.

March 27.

THE least things done for the love of our Divine Master may be full in His sight of the richest and sweetest merit, and the greatest things we may do or suffer, if they are not done in charity, are, as the Apostle says, worth nothing.

March 28.

WE have to expiate the pains due to a world of sins, surpassing all memory ; and as yet we have but little chastised ourselves. There is no time to lose. "So run, that you may obtain."

March 29.

OUR besetting sin is the sin oftenest committed, and with the greatest facility, and the one we forget with the greatest speed—the one from which we turn away our eyes, and for which we try to make excuse before God, and give ourselves Absolution.

———

March 30.

ALL our unrest and weariness is in and of ourselves. It is either the slavery of some tyrannous sin, or the indulgence of some fretful, implacable temper, or some repining discontent at what we are, or some impotent straining after what God has not willed us to be,—these, I say, and only these or such-like, make men weary and desolate.

March 31.

BEWARE of money and the desire for it ; of carefulness and mistrust of God. Labour in your lot ; be content with such things as you have, and be careful for nothing. The only sure investment for our worldly goods is in works of mercy to the poor of Christ.

————

April 1.

A NECESSITY of my reason constrains me to believe the existence of God, because I can in no other way account for my own existence. I am either uncaused, or self-caused, or caused by a cause.

April 2.

I KNOW that I am ; I know that I have
the light of reason, the dictate of conscience, the power of will ; I know that
I did not make all things, nor even myself.
A necessity of my reason compels me to
believe in One higher and greater than I,
from Whom I come, and to Whose image
I am made.

————

April 3.

THERE is no security for perseverance
except in always advancing.   To stand
still is impossible.   A boat ascending a
running stream falls back as soon as it
ceases to advance.   To hold its place is
impossible, unless it gain upon the stream.
So in the spiritual life.

April 4.

BE as sharp as you will with yourselves ; do not bear with the least sin in your own temper ; give no impunity to yourselves or to your own faults.

April 5.

GOD is one in Nature, Christ one in Person, the Church one in organization and singularity of subsistence, depending on its Head, Who is One, and animated by the Holy Ghost, Who is likewise One, the principle of union to the members who constitute the one body by the intrinsic unity of its life.

April 6.

THE handling of holy things without holiness is an awful mystery of condemnation.

April 7.

ARE there none in the noontide of faith and grace who have the heart to build an altar in the midst of their brethren, the poor of Jesus Christ? It would bring you untold blessings. To light one more lamp before the Blessed Sacrament, to rear one more roof above the tabernacle, will enrol you as one of the clouds of witnesses who spread the knowledge of the true God, and of Jesus Christ Whom He has sent.

———

April 8.

LISTEN to God, and answer promptly; lay hold of that grace which is offered to you; keep fast the links of that golden chain; never let it go, and take heed lest you break a link.

April 9.

Do you interpret what befalls you in your life as the overruling, watchful, and loving care of your Divine Friend? If so, you will never murmur, nor repine, nor rebel; you will never chafe against God's providence; you will be content with your lot; you will be ready to thank Him for everything.

April 10.

WE are always unconsciously affecting other men with a power which, could we fully know it, would make us tremble. Our thoughtless actions, random words, unguarded hints, our very tones, even our gestures, in our most relaxed hours, leave impressions on other men such as we neither design nor imagine.

April 11.

HAVE a holy fear of consciously doing anything that may grieve the Holy Spirit; a holy fear of going anywhere, entering into any engagements, amusements, societies, friendships, intimacies, which can come between God and your soul.

April 12.

BY prayer is meant not vocal prayer only, but the prayer of the mind, and of the heart sustained habitually by recollection of the presence of God, and articulated often in silence by desires, aspirations, momentary petitions in the actions and trials of the day.

April 13.

A LOT is meted out to every one of us, and God has chosen it. We do not choose our own lot. Some few of its details we may control; but we no more choose our entire lot than we determine the country or the century in which we are born. It is the providence of God; and He ordains what we shall have, and shall not have; and that lot is given to us, to be content with it, to be satisfied with it, to rejoice in it.

April 14.

IT is but a little time, and we shall all keep Easter in heaven; yet a little while— and what matters a little while of sorrow, of care, toil, or weariness, hardness and solitude, repentance and striving, temptations and patience?

April 15.

AROUND the throne of the kingdom of
the Resurrection we may see by faith those
whom we shall hereafter see in vision—the
Blessed Mother of God, sinless always ; the
beloved disciple, who was without spot ;
Mary Magdalene, once stained through and
through, now white as snow. There they
stand, the type of saints and penitents, in
the kingdom of God, redeemed by the same
Lord and Saviour, washed in the same
precious blood, arrayed in light ; the penitent white as the sinless, because sinless
for ever, for all sins are done away.

April 16.

THERE are three great depths which no
human line can sound—the depth of our
own sinfulness, the depth of our unworthiness, and the depth of our nothingness.

April 17.

THE mind and voice of the Church has never changed, never varied, by an accent or by an iota. As every age has had its heresy, so every heresy has been cast out, some sooner, some later, some with ease, some with difficulty, but all alike are cast out by the vigour of health and life.

April 18.

AFTER the fret and fever of a few short years will come the river of the water of life—"the times of refreshment," and the rest of God. Let us remember that He Who is the Resurrection is always with us; and if we be in Him, all things are ours, all shall be restored to us, all made new, all sinless and deathless, all our own again and for ever.

April 19.

IN the joy of the Resurrection we shall see the countenance of the Friend Who has loved us, sorrowed for us, died for us ; the countenance of the Son of God fixed upon each one of us ; the eyes of our Redeemer looking upon us personally one by one ; His voice speaking to us as He spoke to Mary at the sepulchre, calling us each one by name. This is the beginning of the joy.

April 20.

THE Catholic Church rests not on the judgment of any individual, however holy or wise ; but on the witness of an universal and perpetual body, to which teacher and taught alike are subject ; and because all are in subjection to the Church, all are redeemed from bondage to individual teachers and the authority of men.

April 21.

THE happiness of life, the happiness of home, the happiness of your past, where is it? You have to look back for it; it is gone, or it is going, transient and fleeting; and in a little while it will be no longer. But in the kingdom of God, that life, ever new, of body, of mind, of soul, of home, of happiness, of perfect identity, of mutual recognition, of restored bonds, of love perfected and transfigured in the kingdom of the Resurrection, shall all be changeless and eternal.

April 22.

IF you touch the Cross, it will leave its mark upon you. If you bear no print of the Cross, be sure that you have never touched it yet. Sorrow, humility, self-denial, a tender conscience, a spirit of love, —these are the marks of the Lord Jesus, the print of the nails, and the pledges of our pardon.

April 23.

THE Church teaches that men may be inculpably out of its pale. Now, they are inculpably out of it who are, and have always been, either physically or morally unable to see their obligation to submit to it. And they only are culpably out of it who are both physically and morally able to know that it is God's Will they should submit to the Church ; and, either knowing it, will not obey that knowledge, or, not knowing it, are culpable for that ignorance.

April 24.

THERE is a blessed simplicity in charity, which covereth all things, and hopeth all things. Its very blindness to a brother's faults gives to its touch so delicate a keenness, as to detect the faintest traces of excuse, and the lightest shadow of a good intention.

April 25.

WE may have some years still of temptation, and buffeting, and sorrow, and warfare, and of the Cross on earth. These things may be. Storms upon the lake, clouds upon the mountain,—they are our earthly lot. What matter? If we be children of the Resurrection, heaven is ours. And heaven is near; we know not how long or how soon our day may be.

April 26.

O LET us make up our minds to something; let us be resolved one way or the other; let us be either cold or hot; choose life or death. Choose now and choose wisely, for one false choice may become eternal.

April 27.

LARGER measures of knowledge are a grave stewardship. It is an awful mercy to be greatly exalted—to be highly favoured above other men.

———

April 28.

WHEN the Church suffers anywhere, it is felt everywhere. Every persecution wounds the whole body ; every benediction is a common joy. Because we are members one of another, there is a perfect sympathy binding the whole Church together.

April 29.

IN proportion as we possess sufficient evidence to know the truth, God will require of us to give an account of that truth at the last day. We must give an account both of what we have known and what we have not known, the reason why we have not known that which we might have known.

April 30.

THERE is a sanctity pervading the whole Church, and yet how much of sin attaches *outwardly* to it; how many sinners are within its unity! Our Lord has told us to expect both good fish and bad in the one net, and both tares and wheat in the one field. Such is the mixture of good and evil in the visible Church.

May 1.

THE Author and Finisher of the devotion which the Church perpetuates to the Blessed Mother of God, was Jesus Himself. He founded it by His own example, and taught it to His disciples by His own words and deeds. They who reproach us for the honour we pay to her, reproach Him ; for we have never honoured her so much as He did.

May 2.

THE devotion, or worship, as we say in our Old English speech, to the Blessed Virgin which the Catholic Church teaches to her children, may be best defined in these words : it is the love and veneration which was paid to her by her Divine Son and His disciples, and such as we should have borne to her if we had been on earth with them ; and it is also the love and veneration we shall bear to her next after her Divine Son, when through grace we see Him in His kingdom.

May 3.

THE disciples, from the moment of their call to follow Jesus, learned to know, reverence, and love His Mother. She was the Mother of their Master—of Him Who had spoken to them as never had any man spoken before. His words penetrated and fascinated their hearts with a thrill of awe and love such as no human voice had ever caused till then. He had manifested in their presence alone an honour to His Mother such as He showed to no other.

May 4.

IN no point do we go beyond the devotion of the disciples to Mary; in no point did the devotion of the disciples fall short of ours. No one, not even the Saints of the Church, not even S. Bernard, S. Bonaventure, S. Alphonsus, loved or venerated the Blessed Virgin with a love so tender, a veneration so profound, as S. Peter, S. James, and S. John.

———

May 5.

IF it were true of the poor woman who anointed the head of Jesus, "Wheresoever the Gospel shall be preached that which this woman hath done shall be told for a memorial of her," how much more of her who ministered to Him the substance of His humanity! If the name Mary Magdalene was to be embalmed in the Gospel, how much more the name of His Blessed Mother!

May 6.

FROM the truth of Mary's divine maternity follows her singular and pre-eminent glory; pre-eminent, because never upon any creature was laid a dignity so great as that of bearing the Incarnate God and nurturing Him as her Infant; and singular, because the angels, cherubim and seraphim, are many, and many are the patriarchs, prophets, apostles, and saints; but there was only one Mother of God, because only one Incarnate Son.

————

May 7.

THE "Hail, Mary!" has been the prayer and meditation of saints. All devotion to the Mother of God springs from it, as all harmony springs from the octave. A few notes are the element of all song, as the few words "Hail, full of grace!" are the element of all the love and veneration, the devotion and worship, of the Church for our Blessed Mother.

May 8.

S. Dominic made the " Hail, Mary ! " the measure and the melody of the Rosary of the Incarnation, S. Francis the congratulation of her seven earthly joys, S. Thomas of Canterbury of her seven heavenly joys, S. Philip Benitius the condolence in her seven sorrows. All through the eighteen hundred years of the Church, the " Hail, Mary ! " has been pouring forth its sweetness and its variety like a long strain of endless harmony.

May 9.

The answers to prayer, through the intercession of Mary, in every age of the Church, and in every state of life, and in all manner of trials, public and private, have taught the faithful that she bears an office of power and patronage over us.

May 10.

THEY who are not of the unity of the Church do not believe in the intercession of Mary, because they have never made trial of it.   But the whole Church is pervaded by a consciousness of her love and power now, as it was in the beginning.

May 11.

THE Divine Maternity is the highest glory ever laid upon a creature ; the Immaculate Conception is the grace proportioned to the glory.   Both in grace and glory she is the first of creatures ; for her Son was not a creature, but the Creator.

May 12.

THE dogma of the Immaculate Conception is no more than the final analysis, both in conception and in expression, of the pre-eminent and singular sanctification of the Mother of God.

May 13.

No language can be conceived more ardent or absolute than that in which the earliest records of Christianity, the liturgies, and the early Fathers speak of the Blessed Mother of our Lord. Spotless, sinless, thrice-holy, holier than the seraphim, holiest next after God,—these are the familiar descriptions of her sanctity.

May 14.

I⊤ is certain that if we love God as we ought ; if we bear to our Divine Redeemer tender and grateful hearts ; if we realize the Communion of Saints, and the loving and living relations which bind them to us, and us to them ; if we be conscious of their love to us and their prayers for us ; if we have childlike hearts, holy, loving, and filial towards our heavenly Father ; then it is certain that, next after Jesus, our veneration and our love will be given to her whom He loves with all the filial reverence and all the tender love of His Sacred Heart.

May 15.

BEAR in mind these three things : (1) First, that the Author and Founder of the devotion to the Mother of God is Jesus Himself. (2) Secondly, that the chief promoters of it were the apostles and disciples of our Lord. (3) Thirdly, that in nothing do we go beyond them.

May 16.

To put man and woman upon an equality is not to elevate woman, but to degrade her. I trust that the womanhood of England, to say nothing of the Christian conscience which yet remains, will resist by a stern moral refusal the immodesty which would thrust women from their private life of duty and supremacy into the public conflicts of men.

May 17.

FASHIONS of dress come from some obscure room, in some luxurious and corrupt city, where, by a sort of secret society of folly, rules are laid down, and decrees come forth year after year, which are followed with a servility and, I may say, with a want of Christian matronly dignity, so that the foolish fashion that some foolish person has foolishly invented is propagated all over the civilized countries of Europe. Our forefathers and the women of another age did not bend and undulate with every wind that is wafted over the sea.

———

May 18.

IF we take all things as from God, and behold all things as in the light of the brightness of His coming, all shall be well.

May 19.

READ the rules of life which S. Paul gave to Bishops, Priests, people, parents, children, servants, and homes. Read also what S. Peter counselled as to dress and ornaments. See what the Saints thought, said, and practised even in their childhood, before they had ripened beyond our reach, as to amusements, self-indulgence, and the dangers of the world. These are, or ought to be, the standard of our life.

May 20.

Do not fear to be thought over-strict ; do not fear to be reproached as extreme ; do not fear to be in a minority.

May 21.

I HAVE been often asked whether it is lawful to go to a theatre. My answer has been always, "I cannot forbid you. If you ask what I advise, I say without hesitation, Do not go. I would to God that those who can refrain from such things, as an offering to our Divine Redeemer, would refrain for ever."

May 22.

IT is more generous, it is more in conformity with the example set us by our Divine Lord and Master, to deny ourselves in many things that are lawful. Apply this to dress, to pleasures, to amusements, to the expenditure you make on yourself, to your domestic and private life, and you will find a wide field for its application.

May 23.

OBEDIENCE of domestic life is a great discipline of humility, piety, and self-content. A good son will make a good priest, and a good daughter will make a good nun. A disobedient son will hardly make an obedient priest, and an unloving daughter will hardly make a sister of charity. A good home is a great novitiate.

———

May 24.

THE favour of this world is no sign of the Saints. The Cross is their portion. The voice of the many is no test of truth, nor warrant of right, nor rule of duty. Truth and right, and a pure conscience, have been ever with the few. "Many are called, but few are chosen."

May 25.

CHOOSE your friends from among the friends of God. Be not united with any that are separated from Him ; for they will breathe into your ear, while you are un-conscious, that which will pervade your whole spiritual being.

———

May 26.

THE great sin of us all is creature-worship —putting creatures in the place of God ; and this brings us into bondage. But there is one creature in the world which is the most subtle of all ; there is one crea-ture which is the most fascinating, the most deceitful, which brings men into bondage more than anything else, and that creature is self—the love of self.

May 27.

As the only reality in the world is man, so the only reality in man is his spiritual life. We must strive to be more alone. Solitude and silence are full of reality.

May 28.

WE think that Saints are like the great mountains, or like the cedars of Lebanon, in the kingdom of God—seldom to be seen, and afar off. There are Saints standing amongst us, and we know them not. They do not know it themselves, for sanctity sees only its own imperfections.

May 29.

EDUCATE your children, and promote by all the power you have the Christian education of the children of the poor. The root of society is in the child. The education of the child is the first obligation of the law of God on men.

May 30.

LET us bear in mind this truth—that on the bed of death, and in the day of judgment, to have saved one soul will be not only better than to have won a kingdom, but will overpay by an exceeding great reward all the pains and toils of the longest and most toilsome life.

———

May 31.

JESUS and Mary will to all eternity be Son and Mother, and this one divine fact reveals to us the eternity of our relations. Andrew and Peter, James and John, will be brothers, Martha and Mary sisters, for ever. Our relations are a part of our consciousness ; we could not put them off without spoiling ourselves of the greater part of our personal identity.

June 1.

LEARN to know the love of God in the Sacred Heart of Jesus. It is the Book of Life, open to all, easily to be read. Take that Book of Life and read it, every page. It is written within and without with the pledges and the promises of God's personal love for you.

———

June 2.

IF you would find the Fountain of the Water of Life and the glories of the Eternal Throne, on which the Lord of the Sacred Heart sits and reigns for ever, go into any sanctuary where the light burns silently before the tabernacle. Kneel there and cover your face. Jesus is there, and the Ever-blessed Trinity, and the vision of peace, and the heavenly court, and the kingdom of His glory.

June 3.

THERE is always one Friend in Whom we may find perfect and changeless rest. Other friends often grieve and disappoint us. Our only Divine Friend never fails. We may go to Him at any hour. If He be silent, we know His meaning and His mind. He always welcomes us when we come to Him. He listens to all we say, and He consoles us by listening to our voice; for it is a relief to unburden our soul to a friend, though he answers not a word. We know that we have His sympathy; that He feels with us and for us; that all we say is noted and remembered; and that, if He be silent now, the day is not far off when we shall hear Him say, "Enter thou into the joy of thy Lord."

June 4.

TAKE nothing lower than the Heart of our Divine Lord as the measure and the rule of your own. Do not take any lower standard. Do not take the examples of men. Do not take maxims or motives of your own. Set before you the Sacred Heart in its full and divine perfection.

June 5.

WE who murmur, and repine, and chafe, and fret all the day long if anything goes against us, call ourselves disciples of the Sacred Heart ; and yet we have not so much as the will to bear the Cross, much less to love it.

June 6.

A SPIRIT of reparation draws great graces from the Sacred Heart, and engages all its generosity in our salvation.

June 7.

KEEP as closely as you can to the Sacred Heart of Jesus. Be faithful to His law. Cherish every particle of His truth, every commandment, every counsel of His will, every inspiration of His grace.

June 8.

THROUGH your whole life everything that you do according to the Will of God, being in a state of grace, has in the Book of Remembrance a record, and in the Sacred Heart of our Divine Master a promise of reward, which shall be satisfied at His coming.

June 9.

THE throne of God's sovereignty is the Blessed Sacrament upon the Altar. The Sacred Heart of Jesus Christ, our Lord and King, is there, always reigning, by the power of His love attracting the human will in all its freedom to Himself.

June 10.

THE Holy Ghost reads the heart. Demas "loved this world;" therefore, and for no other reason, he forsook the servants of Jesus Christ.

June 11.

WHAT the dove was at Jordan, and the tongues of fire at Pentecost, that the one visible Church is now: the witness of the mission, advent, and perpetual presence of the Spirit of the Father and of the Son.

June 12.

MAKE up your mind now that not a day shall pass, from this day to your last, without some act of adoration to the Person of the Holy Ghost, without some act of reparation made to Him for your own sins and for the sins of other men. Say day by day the majestic Hymn of the Church, the *Veni Creator Spiritus ;* or that other equally beautiful, and even more full of tenderness, *Veni Sancte Spiritus ;* or say every day, seven times, the *Glori Patri* in honour of the Holy Ghost, to obtain His seven gifts ; raise up your hearts to God, make each of you some short act of reparation and adoration out of the fulness of your soul.

June 13.

WE speak with our Blessed Lord as a friend to friend, face to face, opening our hearts to His Sacred Heart, and conversing with God as with One Who knows all we are by personal experience and human sympathy, and is infinitely pitiful and divinely tender in His love.

June 14.

As we know among ourselves, it is love that awakens love, it is friendship that kindles friendship, it is the sensible manifestation of kindness and of tenderness of heart, of disinterested and self-denying love,—it is this that awakens us to love again ; so is it toward our Lord : He endured all things first, to persuade us to trust in His love.

June 15.

OUR Blessed Lord numbers all the graces you have had, and all the sins you have committed ; take care not to overreach the number allotted to you.

———

June 16.

YOU who have the whole revelation of God, ought to have the whole charity of God in you.   Let your neighbours who are round about, even those who are not of the faith, feel that there is something in you—a warmth, a kindness, a sympathy, and gene-rosity which they find in no other men.

June 17.

UNITE your whole heart, with all its love and all its affections, to our Blessed Lord, to IIis kingdom, to His interests upon earth, to His poverty, to His sufferings, to His contempt, and to His Cross.

———

June 18.

JUST as the Holy Eucharist is always the same in the fulness of its divine sanctity and grace, even though the priest who consecrates and the multitude who receive it be in sacrilege ; and as the light of the sun is always the same, in unchanging splendour, though all men were blind ; so with the truth and sanctity of the Church.

June 19.

WHERESOEVER the Holy Catholic Church is, there is Jesus, reigning in the mystery of the Blessed Sacrament, always near to us; and our union with Him is a union so intimate that the mind cannot define it; the heart alone, illuminated by faith, can know by consciousness that which the intellect cannot comprehend.

June 20.

CORPUS Christi is a second Feast of the Nativity—a Christmas Festival in the summer-tide, when the snows are gone, and flowers cover the earth.

June 21.

THE Blessed Sacrament to sense is bread and wine; to intellect, a symbol; to faith, the Body and Blood of Christ.

June 22.

THERE are only two centres, God and ourselves; and we must rest on one or on the other. We cannot rest on both.

———

June 23.

REPENTANCE is the threshold of the invisible sanctuary, where the Saints are gathering, and here they must fall down before they think to enter. None but they that have either a pure or a broken heart shall see God.

———

June 24.

YOU are all called to be saints; you are, therefore, bound to be saints. Now or hereafter, if you are saved, saints you must be.

June 25.

SOME are scandalized at the mixture of good and evil in the Catholic Church, not knowing the Scriptures, nor believing the Word of God. The mixture of good and evil is permitted in the turbulent sea of this world ; but they shall be separated on the eternal shore. And yet, though there be an evil mixture in the visible Church of Christ—bad Christians, bad Catholics, men whose lives are a scandal and a shame—nevertheless, the sanctity of the Church is never tainted. It depends not on men, but on the Sanctifier.

———

June 26.

AS S. Peter went down to our Blessed Lord upon the water, simply trusting in His power, so must we draw near to Him in our sins, simply trusting in His love.

June 27.

THE Church is imperishable, because its life is God ; indivisibly one, because He is numerically one ; holy, because He is the Fountain of holiness ; infallible both in believing and in teaching, because His illumination and His voice are immutable.

June 28.

To sense the visible Church is a society of men ; to intellect an organized and historical kingdom ; to faith it is the heavenly court on earth, the beginning of the new creation of God.

June 29.

IF there be a visible Church, it is the Church of Rome; and if there be a dogmatic religious truth, it is the Catholic Faith.

———

June 30.

INDIVIDUALS may err, as individuals may die; but the Church cannot err, as the Church cannot die. Because it is the Body of a Divine Head, and that Divine Head is Truth. It is the dwelling-place of the Spirit of Truth, Who, inhabiting the Body, always sustains it in the knowledge and enunciation of truth.

July 1.

WE must seek to have the inward mind of the Church in ourselves. It is not by loud profession of the faith, nor by headlong zeal for truth, nor by eager controversies against error, nor by excited devotions; but by a silent and even life of faith and purity, by a patient following of Christ's footsteps, by a mastery over temper, by mortifying self, by a steady gaze on His mysterious Passion, by being and praying Him to make us like Himself, that we shall bear within us the kingdom and the presence of God.

July 2.

NEXT after God in our love is Mary; infinitely below God, because He alone is the uncreated; immensely above all other creatures, because she is the Mother of God. Being the Mother of Jesus, our Brother, she is our Mother too. Jesus loved her above all creatures, and we cannot be like Him if we do not love her too.

———

July 3.

STRIVE to make your homes to be holy, and your families to be households of saints.

July 4.

IT is the consciousness of the Presence of Jesus, God and man, in the Blessed Sacrament of the Altar, which draws all eyes and all hearts round about Him to the point where He is personally present.

———

July 5.

THERE are three false lights which make us deceive ourselves. (1) The world. We compare ourselves with other people. (2) Kind friends, who are so ready to flatter us. (3) Love of ourselves. We are so tempted to think lightly of our own faults, whilst we are severe with others.

July 6.

WHEN we go to the Altar, we go to the entrance of the world unseen ; to the spot where the visible and invisible worlds unite. The oftener we draw near, the deeper will be our sense of these eternal realities.

———

July 7.

EVERY several Absolution is a royal pardon, freely and abundantly bestowed, not only without money and without any price, but notwithstanding our great unworthiness.

July 8.

THE silver trumpets proclaimed the jubilee once only in every fifty years ; but the Precious Blood cries to us in the Sacrament of Penance at all hours, by day and by night.

———

July 9.

THE Precious Blood of Jesus has brought Absolution upon all men, and for all sins countless as the stars of heaven. There is but one Baptism, but there are many Absolutions ; for the Sacrament of Penance is a fountain ever flowing, perennial and inexhaustible.

July 10.

THE one only sin which is beyond the reach of Absolution, the one only sin which the Precious Blood cannot absolve, is the sin that is not repented of; that is the sole and only sin that shall not be washed as white as snow.

———

' July 11.

WHAT our spirit—that is, our soul—is to our members, that the Holy Ghost is to the members of Christ, to the Body of Christ, which is the Church.

July 12.

IF only we can live in an habitual sense of our perfect pardon and Absolution through the most Precious Blood of Jesus, of His friendship for us, of His perpetual presence, love, and care, we shall have the root of perseverance firmly fixed in our will.

———

July 13.

HAPPINESS is not a thing inherited by the rich alone—the poorest may better have it ; nor is it only for them that have many and dear friends about them—the loneliest may have it in a deeper though a severer measure. For happiness is an inward boon ; it is shed abroad secretly in the heart by the love of Christ.

July 14.

THERE is no sin of any kind, however deep, dark, black as midnight, and often committed, nothing so inveterate, nothing which in the sight of God is so hateful, nothing which to the soul of man is so deadly, that there cannot be Absolution for it in the Sacrament of Penance.

July 15.

S. CHARLES was a mixture of gravity and sweetness, of calmness and of intensity, of invincible courage and exquisite compassion.   It was a character high and stern, yet loving and gentle, severe in its reality and in the majesty of truth.

July 16.

THE Holy Eucharist is Jesus reigning amongst the just, the Sacrament of Penance is Jesus seeking among sinners for those that are lost ; the former is the Sacrament of Saints, the latter of the sinful.

———

July 17.

THERE is but one Absolver, Jesus Christ Himself; but He has ten thousand ministers on earth, through whom He applies His Precious Blood to souls that are truly penitent.

July 18.

GOD alone can absolve, and God alone can give the power of Absolution. When the power of Absolution is exercised by any man, he is but an instrument in the hand of God ; the Absolver is always God Himself.

July 19.

THE Sacrament of Penance is loved by Catholics, and hated by the world. Like the pillar which of old guided the people of God, to us it is all light ; to the world it is all darkness.

July 20.

THE fountain opened in the heavenly Jerusalem for the sin of man is open day and night; always full of power and grace. Jesus Himself is there, the Lord of all power. It is not the first, or one alone, that is healed, but all comers, and all sufferers from all lands, and at all hours; and no man takes away another's Absolution, nor does any one need another's hand to help him to go down into the pool of the most Precious Blood.

July 21.

THERE are four things required in Confession. (1) That the sick man should come. (2) That we should honestly and truly accuse ourselves. (3) That we should tell the truth with sorrow. (4) That we should resolve in coming to sin no more.

July 22.

JESUS is the support of your supernatural life, in sacramental communion as often as you may, in spiritual communion as often as you can, in daily visits to the Presence of Jesus, kneeling in prayer, or sitting at His Feet, as often and as long as the works and hindrances of life will permit.

———

July 23.

WHAT liberty is there so perfect as theirs who, being free from all bondage to creatures, offer their will freely to God, and desire nothing but what He wills for them?

July 24.

THE footprints of God point to a Divine Presence as their only cause. The only Feet which could impress them are those which walked upon the water. For instance, the doctrine of the Holy Eucharist, of the Communion of Saints, of the Church, one, visible, indivisible with its supernatural light and divine infallibility,—all these point to a cause which transcends our reason, as heaven transcends the earth.

———

July 25.

IT is not requiring much of the sinner that he should come and say what is his disease ; that he should show his wounds, and his miseries, and the symptoms of death that are upon him. The physician requires no more for our healing, and he can require no less.

July 26.

MAKE an offering to our Lord in the Blessed Sacrament ; offer yourselves, your life, your love, your heart, your will, your intellect, your liberty, all your actions, all that you are—offer yourself to Him.

————

July 27.

EVEN in a common homely life there are those whom wisdom has made to be the friends of God. Wheresoever they be— the poor mother toiling in her home, the carpenter among his tools, S. Philip in the confessional, S. Charles in the plague-stricken homes of Milan—they are all in the folds of the Divine Presence, in the light and the sweetness of His eternal kingdom.

July 28.

THROUGHOUT our whole life our charity ought to be on the increase ; and if increased, so will be our bliss in eternity.

———

July 29.

OUR tempers, our passions, our inward temptations, our pride and vanity, the self-love and the jealousies and the multitude of inward faults of which we are conscious, will master us little by little, unless we master them.

———

July 30.

FREQUENT Confession and frequent Communion are the two fountains of the knowledge which comes from the experience of the love and tenderness of God in Jesus Christ.

July 31.

WE may *profess* great things cheaply, but it costs dear to *do* and to *suffer* them.

―――

August 1.

RITUAL is seemly and proportionate as the clothing of Truth; but where the reality is present, we become as unconscious of Ritual as of the light of day, or of the circulation of the blood.

―――

August 2.

THE Church in the midst of the world is the bush that burned with fire, and was not consumed. The stem of the bush is enveloped in flame; and the fire which is winding about it spreads through every branch, and reaches to every spray; but the bush is imperishable because it is of God.

August 3.

WHERE the Spirit is, there is the soul of the Church ; and where the Church is, there is the body of the Spirit and all grace.

August 4.

THERE have been in your life times and seasons, sometimes in joy, sometimes in sorrow, sometimes in prayer, sometimes in solitude, sometimes in the midst of the world, when there has come down almost a sensible sweetness to your taste, almost a perceptible fragrance in your thoughts. And what is this sweetness and fragrance ? It is the Divine Presence scattering abroad "the benedictions of sweetness."

August 5.

WHEN you find the world most opposed to you, be of good cheer ; you have a sure token that you are in the right. It has been so always—it always will be. S. Ignatius was never sad except when the world prospered him, and never so glad and buoyant as when he received the promise that his sons should be ever hated for the Name of Jesus.

August 6.

THE errors of individuals cannot prevail against the Church. Individuals depend on the Church, not the Church on individuals. The Church depends on its Divine Head, and upon the perpetual presence of the Divine Person, the Holy Ghost, Who inhabits it.

August 7.

LET us offer ourselves up to Christ, to be disposed of as He sees best, whether for joy or sorrow, blessing or chastisement; to be high or low; to be slighted or esteemed; to be full, or to suffer need ; to have many friends, or to dwell in a lonely home ; to be passed by, or called to serve Him and His kingdom in our own land or among people of a strange tongue ; to be, to go, to do, to suffer even as He wills, even as He ordains, even as Christ endured.

August 8.

BY your Baptism you are pledged to a life of sanctity. The life of Christ is your example. Your calling is to be ever growing in likeness to the Son of God.

August 9.

WHERE there is a calm inward shining of the love of God, there is contentment and a submissive will, and a glad content in our present lot.

———

August 10.

EVERY man must bear his own burden when the secrets of all hearts shall be revealed. A humble confession strives to anticipate the hour of isolated trial, and to fall down alone as guilty before the judgment-seat of Christ.

August 11.

THE Saints reflect our Lord each one in his way and measure ; and their conformity arises from a double power of assimilation—from contemplation and communion ; contemplation, by which He illuminates and informs His servants with His own mind and example ; communion, by which He dwells in them, pervades them with His substance, changes them into the likeness of His Sacred Heart.

———

August 12.

S. VINCENT of Paul used to say, "If we had one foot in heaven, yet, if we ceased to mortify ourselves before we could draw the other after it, we should be in danger of losing our soul."

August 13.

INDIVIDUALS and nations may fall from unity as from sanctity; but unity as a divine institution stands secure. Unity is changeless, whosoever falls; unity does not admit of degrees.

———

August 14.

HUMILITY can never be cast down while it has hope, and hope can never be presumptuous while it has humility.

August 15.

MARY stands at the right hand of her Son, Who stands at the right hand of IIis Father; and the right hand of her Son is almighty. And the prayers of His Blessed Mother never fail. They never fail, because she never asks amiss; they never fail, because she knows the Will of her Divine Son. The Immaculate Heart of Mary intimately knows the Sacred Heart of Jesus.

August 16.

WE cannot be too humble, and we cannot be too hopeful; and when humility and hope are joined together, hope sustains humility, and humility chastens hope.

August 17.

THIS present hour is all we have. To-morrow must be to-day before we can use it ; and day after day we squander in the hope of a to-morrow ; but to-morrow shall be stolen away too, as to-day and yesterday. It is *now* we must be penitent, *now* we must be holy. This hour has its duty, which cannot be done the next. To-morrow may bring its own opportunities, but will not restore to-day's. The convictions of this hour, if unheeded, will never come back. God may send others, but these will be gone for ever.

August 18.

IT is impossible for us to make the duties of our lot minister to our sanctification without a habit of devout fellowship with God. This is the spring of all our life, and the strength of it. It is prayer, meditation, and converse with God that refreshes, restores, and renews the temper of our minds at all times, under all trials, and after all conflicts and contacts with the world.

————

August 19.

EVERY substance casts its shadow, and every truth leaves its definite impression upon the reason of man ; and the enunciation of that definite impression is dogma.

August 20.

JUDAS is an example how a soul once innocent may be slowly changed into the worst sin, and even at last fall, with little intention of committing the whole evil which follows from its act.

August 21.

LET us by prayer and self-chastisement so cross and keep under our likings, preferences, views, opinions, judgment in all things, when the will of the Church is made known, that we may in all things obey "as unto the Lord, and not unto men."

August 22.

THE very strength and life of all self-discipline is order, certainty, and decision. Our true safeguard against temptation is to be the same at all times, in all companies, in all places ; not to vary and adapt ourselves to the humour of others, thereby adopting their temptations with their habits, but to be always and everywhere ourselves, and to oppose to the temptations of the world the consistency of a matured and practised habit of self-control.

August 23.

THERE grew up in the world the true vine and the branches—the one world-wide organization; the one life-giving society of men, united by baptism, faith, and worship; by submission to one Authority; by the recognition of one visible Head—the sole Fountain of supernatural knowledge and supernatural power.

————

August 24.

CEREMONIES are a mere mask to the unbelieving and the undevout. They are the folds of the Divine Presence, the countenance of the unseen Majesty to those that believe and love.

August 25.

OUR everyday life abounds in manifold opportunities of self-discipline ; we shall find them in the hours of prayer, in the practice of charity, in almsdeeds, in fasting, in abstinence, in straitening our ease, in abstaining from lawful and, to ourselves, expedient things for others' sakes, in curbing our pleasures, in bearing slander, in forgiving injuries, in obeying our superiors, in yielding to our equals, in giving up our liberty for the good of others, in crossing the daily intentions of our will.

August 26.

WHEREINSOEVER you resolve to forsake anything for Christ's sake, bear the trial patiently, and wait for the end. There must be some irksomeness, nay, some galling edge, some burden in our yoke, or we have need to look well lest we be carrying a mere mocking shadow of His Cross.

August 27.

REMEMBER God, forget yourselves, and forget yourselves in remembering God.

August 28.

THE loving compassion, active emotion of pity, the tears and tenderness with which the holiest men have ever dealt with the sinful, is a proof that, in proportion as sin loses its power over them, their sympathy with those that are afflicted by its oppressive yoke becomes more perfect.

August 29.

SINNERS put the worst construction on each other's words and acts. They have no consideration or forbearance. Their apparent sympathy is but a fellowship in the same disobedience. And so also the sympathy of the world; how hollow, formal, and constrained it is ! How little soothing or consoling in our sorrows and trials are worldly friends, even the kindest-hearted of them ! And why, but because it is peculiarly the property of true sanctity to be charitable ? And in the grace of charity is contained gentleness, compassion, tenderness of hand in touching the wounds of other men, fair interpretations, large allowances, ready forgiveness.

August 30.

OUR life from first to last teaches us this lesson : it is one continuous whole, gathering up itself through all its course, and perpetuating its earliest features in its latest self; the child is in the boy, the boy is in the man, the man is himself for ever.

———

August 31.

COUNT all things loss, that you may win the truth, without which the inheritance of God's kingdom is not ours. Labour for it, and weary yourselves until you find it ; and forget not that if your religion be indefinite, you have no true knowledge of your Saviour ; and if your belief be uncertain, it is not the faith by which we can be saved.

September 1.

IF the first hour of every day were spent in the presence, certain though unseen, of our guardian Angel, or of our patron Saint, our whole day would be restrained and elevated by it.

September 2.

ANGELS' hands have been about you from the waters of Holy Baptism. Their guidance, unseen, unfelt, has drawn you again and again from ills which your hearts had chosen. In seasons of weakness they have stayed you up; in the hour of wavering they have kept you from falling.

September 3.

SATAN knows well that if he can separate religion from instruction, he has cut through the roots of the Christian civilization of the world.   For that reason all the art, all the wiles, all the frauds, all the false politics of this day, are directed to what is called secular education, national education, imperial education—anything you like, only not Christian education.

September 4.

THE widow's cake and the widow's mite, and the cup of cold water, and the spices that were bought, but never needed, for Jesus was already risen ; and every kind word, and gentle tone, and loving watch-fulness in little things, by which the humblest and most homely life is turned to gold, and transfigured in secret before God and the guardian Angels ;—all these shall have a measure of bliss and glory which the world cannot conceive, because it seeth not the Holy Ghost, neither knoweth Him.

September 5.

WHATEVER else we forego, we may not forego our prayers ; whatever else is at our will to give up, this is not ; however necessary we may think other things, this is the thing needful above all ; our work must be done, and yet our devotions must not be left undone.

———

September 6.

PERFECT beings may be tempted as the Angels ; and sinless beings as Adam in the garden, Christ in the wilderness.

September 7.

IF we love God with a love of apprecia-
tion above all persons and things created,
nothing will draw us from His will.   This
effective love may be calm, and with little,
if any, sensible emotion ; but it reigns in the
soul, and governs the life in deed, word,
and thought, restraining from all that God
condemns, and prompting to all that God
commands or wills.

September 8.

As the worship we pay the Blessed Virgin is infinitely less than the Divine worship which is due to God only, but immensely greater than the worship we pay to all the Saints—for the Saints are innumerable, but the Mother of God is one—and as the throne on which she sits is lower by infinite space than the throne of God, but higher by an immensity than all the thrones in the heavenly court, so the gift of piety offers to her continually a love and adoration which is beyond all that we pay or is due to all the Saints.

September 9.

ALL the day long our life and lot are full of opportunities of doing good, and we allow them to pass away.   They are golden opportunities, like the seed-time and the harvest, which, with all their treasures, pass with the year and return no more.

September 10.

WE receive grace as a hundred, and we correspond as twenty; or we receive as twenty, and correspond as one.

September 11.

GOD looks in compassion on our heavy hours and mournful days, our secret indignation, our shame which burns inwardly, our bruised and trembling hearts.

September 12.

THERE was never any one whose life was fuller of endless employments, or more broken by countless interruptions, than the life of our Blessed Lord. This may show us that the most laborious may be the holiest of Saints.

September 13.

THOUGH martyrdom by the scaffold or the sword be past, there are other martyrdoms to be suffered.   There is the martyrdom of charity in the pestilence, the martyrdom of zeal in wearing our life and strength for the souls of men ; there is the martyrdom of a will, prompt and ready for life or for death, in behalf of the truth and the Church.

September 14.

OUR character is our will ; for what we *will* we *are*.

September 15.

How many spring-times and seed-times have we lost ! how many a summer is past without a harvest ! how many an autumn without a vintage !

September 16.

OBEDIENCE to the Will of God is a work of direct and simple consciousness. It is to be wrought in us by its own self-confirming power. It is by doing the Will of God ; by recognizing it in all the changes of life ; by reading the expression of the Divine mind in the course of this troubled world ; by bowing ourselves down before it under whatsoever guise it may reveal itself; by yielding ourselves in gladness of mind both to do and suffer it ; counting it a holy discipline, and a loving correction of our own wilfulness, by praying Him never to stay His Hand till the power and will of self be abolished from our regenerate being.

September 17.

WATCH over the changes and inclinations of your will, for every one bears upon eternity.   Every energy lays in another touch upon your deepening character; every moment fixes its colours with a greater steadfastness.

———

September 18.

Do your little duties, which most men make light of, with great exactness; for if you will faithfully do your lesser duties, your greater duties, I may say, will take care of themselves.

September 19.

Do not be out of heart at the ever-present consciousness of the weakness of your mortal nature. It is well known, and better understood, and more closely scanned by Him, to Whose perfection you are intimately united. Our weakness and our faults are left to abide in us, that we may learn the perfection of hating what God abhors.

———

September 20.

ALAS for the man that is too busy to pray, for he is too busy to be saved! Alas for us! What would they judge those Saints of old, who wore the very stones with their perpetual kneeling?

September 21.

How shall any one who knows himself to be a simple expression of the Will of God, together with a little dust from the earth, have confidence in self?

———

September 22.

THERE are two things which are never apart—perfect sanctity and perfect unity; and these are as the two witnesses of God, which stand beside "the truth as it is in Jesus."

September 23.

EVERY man has his own particular character, and every character its own particular cast. We have our characteristic faults, and our characteristic weakness. Beware of those particular forms of temptation which have already once held you in their power, or sapped your better resolutions.

———

September 24.

WHO knows what graces he has lost, and may be losing at this moment, from want of aspiration?

September 25.

THE most precious thing we have, next to grace, is time; and we owe an account of our time, as we owe an account of our grace.

———

September 26.

WE may learn, from our Blessed Lord's temptation in the wilderness, that it is no sin to be tempted; nor is our being tempted any proof of our being sinful. This is a most consolatory thought; for, among the afflictions of life, few are so bitter and perpetual as temptation. Sorrows, pains, disappointments, crosses, oppositions, are not to be compared in suffering to the inward distress of being tempted to evil deeds, words, desires, and thoughts.

September 27.

REMEMBER always that the things of God must be done in God's way.

September 28.

EVERY duty, even the least duty, involves the whole principle of obedience; and little duties make the will dutiful, that is, supple and prompt to obey. Little obediences lead into great. "He that is faithful in that which is least is faithful also in much."

September 29.

EXTERNAL splendour of worship is good, but internal truth and reality in the worship of God is better.

———

September 30.

THE softness, and the glare, and the temptations, and the licence, and the lax examples that are about us, are more seducing and dangerous than the winter of penal laws. They hardened the man-hood of Catholic parents. The summer sun relaxes many.

October 1.

AT no time is the protection of Angels and the help of God more near to us than when "the blast of the mighty is like a whirlwind beating against a wall."

——————

October 2.

IF we choose God above all things, and break with the world, we shall have our share in the Cross ; but we shall bless God for it in all its forms, knowing it to be the pledge of His love and care.

October 3.

A SOUL has an endless capacity : either of bliss, which is the participation of the beatitude of God ; or of an agony which the heart of man cannot conceive.

———

October 4.

HOLY fear, filial piety, and fortitude form the perfection of children of the poor, and of the poor in spirit, such as S. Francis, S. Philip, S. Charles.

October 5.

THE most perfect prayers are those of Saints and of little children, because in both there is the same freedom from the hard, unconcerned, self-contemplative habit of mind which besets the common sort of Christians, and the same presence of awe, tenderness of conscience, simplicity and truth.

———

October 6.

BE this our one end in life, to cleanse our hearts, that we may behold more and more of the beauty and the splendour of the Divine Presence, that we may see God in all His creatures, in all His providence, in all the events and changes, and the calls and chastisements of life.

October 7.

YOUR place, your crown, your ministry in God's unseen kingdom, are all marked out for you.

———

October 8.

THE unity and universality of Christianity and of the Church in which it was divinely incorporated, and of Christendom which the Church has created, exclude and convict, as new, fragmentary, and false, all forms of Christianity which are separate and local.

October 9.

WE are answerable not only for what we know, but for what we might know. Whensoever the light comes within the reach of our sight, or the voice within the reach of our ear, we are bound to follow it, to inquire and to learn ; for we are answerable not only for what we can do by absolute power now, but for what we might do if we used all the means we have ; and therefore, whensoever the Church of God comes into the midst of us, it lays all men under responsibility.

October 10.

BE always beginning ; never think that you can relax, or that you have attained the end.

October 11.

THE life of our Lord exhibits to us the most perfect example of constant employ-ments. If anything in it be prominent, it is the multitude of works, the never-ending service of all that came or sent for Him, in sick chambers, in homes of sorrow, in synagogues, in Pharisees' houses, in the temple, in the mid-stream of men.

———

October 12.

THERE are two lessons taught us by all the Saints of God.   The one is, that they and we, Religious and Secular, as our names may be, are bound, by law of our supernatural existence, to love each other's perfection ; the other is, that we rejoice in each other's works.

October 13.

OUR hidden life with God is the very soul of our spiritual being in our own home, in the Church, and in the world.

October 14.

THERE are few more thrilling words in Holy Scripture than these : " There are just men and wise men, and their works are in the hand of God, and yet man knoweth not whether he be worthy of love or hatred."

October 15.

To stand apart from the throng of earthly things, and to let them hurry by as they will, and whither they will, is the only sure way to calmness and clearness in the spiritual life.

———

October 16.

THERE can be no real fear, or reverence, or seriousness of heart, until a man has come to understand, at least in some measure, what he is ; that is, to realize his own awful structure and destiny.

October 17.

IT is by living much alone with God, by casting off the burden of things not needful to our inner life, that we become familiar with the world unseen.

———

October 18.

ONE mind and one will fuses and holds in perfect unity the whole multitude of the faithful throughout all ages, and throughout all the world.

October 19.

WE are most liable to temptation at times when we think ourselves least likely to be overcome; when things have been going on smoothly; when we have been long unmolested by assaults. There are times when we have need to watch with tenfold care, lest, through our slackness of security, peace should be more dangerous to us than temptation.

———

October 20.

THE least act of pure love is more precious in God's sight than a whole ocean of charitable works and contributions which are mixed up and debased by worldly fashion, excitement, and self in its thousand forms.

October 21.

THERE are two things which God hates, backsliding and lukewarmness; and there are two which He will avenge, an alienated heart and a will at war with His.

———

October 22.

IF we take all things as from God, and behold all things as in the light of the brightness of His coming, all shall be well.

October 23.

WE are sent into this world, that by our own will and choice we should deter-mine our eternal portion. Our eternal state will be no more than the carrying out of what we are now.

———

October 24.

WHAT a life is ours! We serve God by fits and by starts; we have cold fits and hot fits, like men in an ague, like those that are struck by fever; sometimes we are in earnest, sometimes we give up; we are carried away by gusts of temptation; a frown of the world will kill off all our good resolutions. Such is our life! perpetually tossed to and fro like waves of the sea.

October 25.

FORWARDNESS is a part of the lawless-
ness of these days, and shows a decline
of the finer instincts of womanhood, and
a loss of that decisive Christian conscience
which can distinguish not only between
what is right and wrong, but between what
is dignified and what is undignified both
for woman and for man.

October 26.

THE friends that love you and speak
fair and soft things to you are not friends
compared to those who look upon you
with sharp eyes, and speak with cold
voices, and bear unkind hearts. They
try what you are ; they try your patience,
the spirit of your humility—whether you
have a crucified will, which is the sure
mark of the true disciple of Jesus Christ.

October 27.

THE will fell by the unbelief of Eve, the first virgin, and was restored through the faith of Mary, the second Virgin. The first Eve listened to the tempter, and fell; the second Eve listened to the angel, and believed.

———

October 28.

GOD attracts us to Him by instincts, and desires, and aspirations after a happiness higher than sense, and more enduring, more changeless, than this mortal life. God speaks to us articulately in the stirring life of nature, and the silence of our own being.

October 29.

To doubt of God's love brings winter into the soul ; to feel it feebly and faintly is as the cloudy and churlish sky, which hinders the ripening influence of the light.

October 30.

REMEMBER that falls are not always by the grosser sins which the world takes count of, but by spiritual sins, subtle and secret, which leave no stain upon the outward life.

October 31.

LET us read the traces of God's loving Hand in all our ways—in all the events, the changes, the chances of this troubled state. It is God that dispenses all.

———

November 1.

THE Saints, by their intercession and their patronage, unite us with God. They watch over us, they pray for us, they obtain graces for us. Our guardian Angels are round about us. The man who has not piety enough to ask their prayers must have a heart but little like to the love and veneration of the Sacred Heart of Jesus.

November 2.

THE Catholic Church, the true Mother of souls, cherishes with loving memory all her departed. Never does a day pass but she prays for them at the altar; never does a year go by that there is not a special commemoration of her children departed, on one solemn day, which is neither feast nor fast, but a day of the profoundest piety and of the deepest veneration.

November 3.

How different all will look upon a death-bed ! Then a new and true light will reveal a multitude of secrets, and show much that we never believed possible. How different all will appear when we look back upon our earthly life from the world beyond the grave in the hour of the particular judgment, and at the moment of entering Purgatory, and at the general judgment of the last day ! Then all masks shall be taken off from all faces, and we shall know as we are known, and see as we are seen. Then many who have seemed to know each other—parents, children, friends, pastors, penitents—shall know each other for the first time, and wonder at the vain show in which they lived and died.

November 4.

S. CHARLES teaches all men that their work is what they are; that to do one thing and to be another is impossible; that if they would teach men to serve God, they must do His Will; if they would bring souls to contrition, they must live in penance.

November 5.

SHRINK from no sorrow, so it be purifying. Our evils and our sins lie so deep, they must needs be long in the refiner's fire. Pray rather that, if need be, you may be tried seven times, so that all may be clean purged out.

November 6.

As we die so shall we be—our character running on into eternity. The bent, disposition, inclination of the soul, with all its powers and affections, shall endure, and abide with us for ever; with this only change—that we shall be either better or worse, for good or for evil, absolute and changeless.

———

November 7.

O WHAT an hour, when God shall come, and all His holy Angels, and all the children of the kingdom—all who have loved, served, waited, suffered for Him— the first and the last—all in perfect sameness, recognition, bliss, and splendour; their raiment white and glistening, and their countenance as the sun shineth in his strength !

November 8.

THAT in us which shall never die is changing daily, is being moulded or marred according as we yield to or resist the working of His Word and Spirit—is taking the eternal stamp of good or ill.

November 9.

ALL depends on perseverance. Without this nothing avails. The grace and perfection and splendour of the Angels could not save them. The daily fellowship with Jesus, His doctrines and miracles, and three years of His presence, did not save Judas. The gift of regeneration, and of the sacraments of grace, were all in vain to Ananias and Sapphira. All alike lacked one thing, and that one thing lacking lost them all things. They had not perseverance; and though they had everything else, nothing without this was of any avail.

November 10.

How carelessly men treat themselves! They live as if they had no souls. In their traffic of this life they scheme as if they were to live for ever. In their preparation for death they trifle as if there were no life beyond the grave.

————

November 11.

FEARFUL thought! we were born alone, and alone we must die; and yet through all our life we, as it were, flee from loneliness, which is alike the beginning and the ending of our earthly transit.

November 12.

GOD knows from all eternity who will be saved, and how many they will be. He does not diminish the number by refusing salvation to the willing; and He will not multiply the number by forcing the free will of those who will not believe.

November 13.

TRULY, to know what we are before God, we must take our whole life, with its context, and read it in the light of God's love and providential care. Guilt is a complex thing—a balance of many particulars on God's part and on ours. It is our sins multiplied by His mercies; our transgressions by His gifts of light and grace.

November 14.

REMEMBER that no penitent soul can perish. And no soul that loves God can be lost.

———

November 15.

WE shall be tried by that which we have known and done ; and we shall be compelled to lay our hand upon our mouth, and to confess that in all our life we never did evil, in thought, word, or deed, but we might have refrained from doing it, and might have done good instead if we had had the will ; that every act of evil was a free act, and an irrational and immoral abuse of our will.

November 16.

A sign of mental obedience is devotion to the Saints. They are our examples. Their counsels, their sayings, their instincts, are our rule and admonition. S. Philip bids us read authors who have S. before their name.

———

November 17.

Many of the Saints, as S. Charles, confessed every day. We wonder what they could find to accuse themselves of. It was because they were Saints that they saw so much where we see so little.

November 18.

THE fall of Demas is near to us all. He was weary of the Apostolic life, of labours, watchings, and fastings. It was a life of counsels ; the life of the commandments was enough for such as he. How fair and reasonable all this appears ; how like the reasoning and the lives of many at this day !

———

November 19.

EVERY substance in the world has its shadow ; you cannot separate the shadow from the substance. Where the substance moves, the shadow follows. So every sin has its pain ; it matters not whether we think of it or no, whether we believe it or no.

November 20.

WE may fast in the midst of the world, in its business and distractions, even when compelled to be present in the midst of its feastings. Let it be a matter between ourselves and God.

————

November 21.

LIVE as you would wish to die, because as you die, so you will be to all eternity. Precisely that character which you have woven for yourself through life, by the voluntary acts of free will, be it for good or for evil, that will be your eternal state before God. As the tree falls, so shall it be. Make one mistake, and that mistake is made for ever.

November 22.

EVERY good action has a merit, that is, a certain conformity to the Will of God ; and every evil action has a merit, that is, a deformity, which will be followed by punishment.

———

November 23.

As there is a heaven, so there is a hell. As there is eternal life, so there is eternal death. If there be a God Who is holy, just, pure, true, and unchangeable, then, if man is impure, unjust, unholy, and false, and will not change by repentance, God and that soul cannot unite in eternity.

November 24.

THERE is no sin that has ever been committed that has not been followed by its measure of judicial pain. It must be some day expiated, either by bearing it here or bearing it hereafter; or by a loving sorrow prevailing with God, through the Precious Blood of Jesus Christ, to wash out from the book of His remembrance that great debt of accumulated sin.

November 25.

IT is so easy for men to be lost. Look back only on your own life. It has been perhaps chequered all along alternately with states of sin and states of grace. It may be there have been seasons of mortal sin only for a day, in which, if God had cut us off before the sun went down, salvation would have been impossible to all eternity.

November 26.

EVERY wound borne now will be glorified, every stigma will have its radiance, and every sorrow will be turned into joy, when, through the perseverance of fortitude, all who have suffered with our Lord shall reign with Him in His kingdom.

November 27.

STRIVE to live in a perpetual readiness to die ; and this you will attain, if you learn to love our Lord's Presence now.

November 28.

BETTER, far better, to wear now " in the body the marks of the Lord Jesus," that we may be arrayed at the last day in white raiment, than to be full of the gifts of this life, to be served and worshipped by the world, and at that day to stand before His piercing eyes, naked and defiled, and all men see our shame.

November 29.

IT will be a day of reversing many an unequal lot, when Christ shall distribute the rewards of His kingdom, not according to our thoughts and judgments, but according to the spiritual and universal condition by which He has proved His own elect. "Many that are first shall be last, and the last first."

November 30.

ANY suffering in this world, rather than to perish in the world to come. Any shame now, rather than shame before Christ at His coming with the Holy Angels.

———

December 1.

THEOLOGIANS teach that many belong to the Church who are out of its visible unity. As a moral truth, to be out of the Church is no personal sin except to those who sin in being out of it. That is, they will be lost, not because they are *geographically* out of it, but because they are *culpably* out of it.

December 2.

ONE of the chief reasons why we find it so hard to pray, one of the chief causes of our distraction, wandering, and all in-devotion, is the infrequency and shortness of our prayers.

———

December 3.

FORTITUDE has three signs by which it may be known. The first is silence under pain : " Jesus held His peace." The second is meekness: " He opened not His mouth." The third is gladness under wrongs : Peter and John rejoiced that they were counted worthy to suffer for the Name of Christ.

December 4.

THEY who recognize, by the light of faith, the sovereignty of God in all things, will recognize the sovereignty of God in the daily and hourly details of their own personal life and in the changes of their lot.

———

December 5.

No sin can be small which is a great offence against a great God—against a great majesty, a great authority, a great purity, a great justice, a great truth. No; not the least venial sin that was ever committed can be absolved but through the Precious Blood which was shed upon the Cross. Little sins ! God have mercy on those who talk this language !

December 6.

STEADILY live up to the light you possess. The light you already have is great, and great, therefore, must be your obedience.

December 7.

THE grace of the Holy Ghost is in you ; and grace is better than life, as the soul is precious above the body, and eternity above time. Grace is the finger of God upon the soul.

December 8.

THE first and, till then, the greatest work of the new creation was the singular and pre-eminent sanctification, or immaculate conception, of the Blessed Mother of God. She was the firstfruits of the Holy Ghost ; the only soul, since the innocence of the first Adam and of the first Eve in Paradise, on whom original sin had never cast its shadow.

December 9.

O WONDER of love, O Friend all gentle, all pure, all wise, in Whose Presence to abide, under Whose loving gaze to dwell, is heaven—shall we indeed see Thy beauty? O Love, greater than love of man, Love of God, Love eternal, which created me, suffered for me, died for me, bare with me in my long, blind, stubborn rebellions, spared, shielded, restrained, converted me by holy inspirations and the pleadings of tender upbraiding—do I now see Thee face to face ?

December 10.

FERVOUR consists in these three things— regularity, punctuality, and exactness. That is, doing our duty to God by rule ; doing it punctually at the right time ; and exactly, that is, as perfectly as we can.

December 11.

IN the true Paradise there shall be no seasons nor vicissitudes; no sweat of the face, nor hard toil for bread. An ever-lasting noontide shall be there; an endless spring in the newness of unfading joy; a perpetual autumn in the ripeness of its gifts.

December 12.

THE severest life without a conscious choice is less than the least acts of self-impoverishment with a clear and single aim of foregoing something that we may find it in His kingdom.

December 13.

NONE have more cause to fear than those who are fearless in such a world and in such a warfare; for none are more in danger than those who think they are safe.

———

December 14.

IF God has given you the perfect illumination of faith, He has laid on you the obligation of having the largest and most perfect charity towards those that are disinherited of the great heirloom which you have received.

December 15.

THE love of God *super omnia* in that measure detaches the heart from creatures, and they who are detached from creatures are liberated from a manifold bondage.

December 16.

IT is by living in our plain path of duty, but with an habitual remembrance of the coming of our Lord ; by using the world as we use our daily food, not so much from choice as from necessity, and yet with no unthankful sullenness, but with gladness, and singleness of heart ; by being ever ready, both for the duties of the day and for the coming hour of judgment ;—by this twofold discipline of self a true Christian is so prepared, that the day of Christ can neither come too late nor too soon for him·

December 17.

THE most fearful and wonderful of mysteries is man. To be ever changing, and yet to be immortal; that, after this changeful life ended, there should be life everlasting, or the worm that dieth not, bespeaks some deep counsel of God, some high destiny of man.

———

December 18.

IF the heart be right with God, He will weigh the rest in a balance of compassion.

December 19.

WHEN the heart is united with God, all its first acts are benign. A heart full of charity makes a head full of just interpretations and of kindly judgments.

———

December 20.

WHAT is it that keeps us perpetually straining and moiling and wearing ourselves away, but some desire which is not chastened, some thought of the heart which is not dead to this worldly state? What makes us lament the flight of time and the changes of the world, but that we are still a part of it, and share its life? What makes us die so hard, but that we leave behind us more treasures than we have laid up in heaven; that our hearts are not there, but here?

December 21.

THOSE that love God can never imagine for Him any perfection of love and tenderness which goes beyond the truth, or even reaches towards the exceeding depth of His compassion. To those who love Him, God is a perpetual Object of loving contemplation ; and as He is contemplated, He is more and more perfectly known with the knowledge which comes by the heart.

———

December 22.

As the thermometer tells the measure of heat or cold, so our sanctification goes onward or backward, just in proportion as we mortify ourselves.

December 23.

THE Council of Trent teaches that God never forsakes any one who does not forsake Him first; secondly, that if we forsake Him it is our own free act; and thirdly, that our own act is by our own free will, so that if we fail of eternal life it is by our own wilful fault.

———

December 24.

IT would make us all fervent if, when we go to the Altar, we were to say, "This may be my *last* Communion;" or, in our Confession, "This may be my *last* Absolution."

December 25.

SENSE beheld in Jesus of Nazareth a man ; intellect, a man endowed with supernatural powers ; faith, the Word made flesh.

———

December 26.

A FATHER of the desert was one day asked in vision whether he would desire to see a soul more perfect than himself. He was carried to a poor home, where he saw a mother toiling for her children. It was a humble likeness of the Holy House ; and under that roof were cares, anxieties, weariness, privations, labour, self-denials, glad submission of will, tenderness of affection, pity and service, and filial piety to God. These things are a discipline of perfection, which subdue the heart and keep it humble before God and man.

December 27.

NONE ever graced a marriage-feast as He Who knew not the very taste of earthly happiness. None was ever so meek, gentle, and benign as He that was alive to God alone.

———

December 28.

LITTLE children, in their innocence, which is akin to the sanctity of God, are wiser than all their teachers, and have understanding above their elders.

December 29.

BETTER or worse we must perforce grow to be : nearer to the mind of Christ, or further from the fellowship of God.

———

December 30.

O BLESSED hour, after all the sorrows, and wrongs, and falsehoods, and darkness, and burdens of life, to see God face to face ; to be made sinless with an exceeding strength ; to be as the light, in which there "is no darkness" !   Be this our hope, our chiefest toil, our almost only prayer.

December 31.

WHAT matter, then, a little pain, a little sorrow, a little penance, a few crosses, if, after a little while, there be an inheritance of eternal joy?

PRINTED BY WILLIAM CLOWES AND SONS, LIMITED,
LONDON AND BECCLES.

www.ingramcontent.com/pod-product-compliance
Lightning Source LLC
Chambersburg PA
CBHW030557040726
47497CB00008B/2768